Calvin Can't Fly

The Story of a Bookworm Birdie

by Jennifer Berne

illustrated by Keith Bendis

STERLING CHILDREN'S BOOKS

New York

Calvin is a starling.

He was born under the eaves of an old barn with his three brothers, four sisters, and sixty-seven thousand four hundred and thirty-two cousins.

Starlings have BIG families.

Right from the beginning Calvin was different . . . right from the day all the little starlings tumbled out of their nests to discover the world.

Charlie discovered worms.

Adeline discovered grass.

Clement discovered dirt.

Aubrey discovered water.

And Calvin . . . well, Calvin discovered a BOOK.

While all of Calvin's cousins chased beetles, bugs, and ants,

Calvin was learning to read letters, words, and sentences.

At night, his cousins dreamed of insect eating and garbage picking.

Calvin dreamed of adventure stories, legends, and poetry.
He even dreamed that someday he'd become a great writer himself.

On June first, when all the little starlings lined up for flying lessons with their teacher, Mr. Wingstead, Calvin was nowhere to be seen.

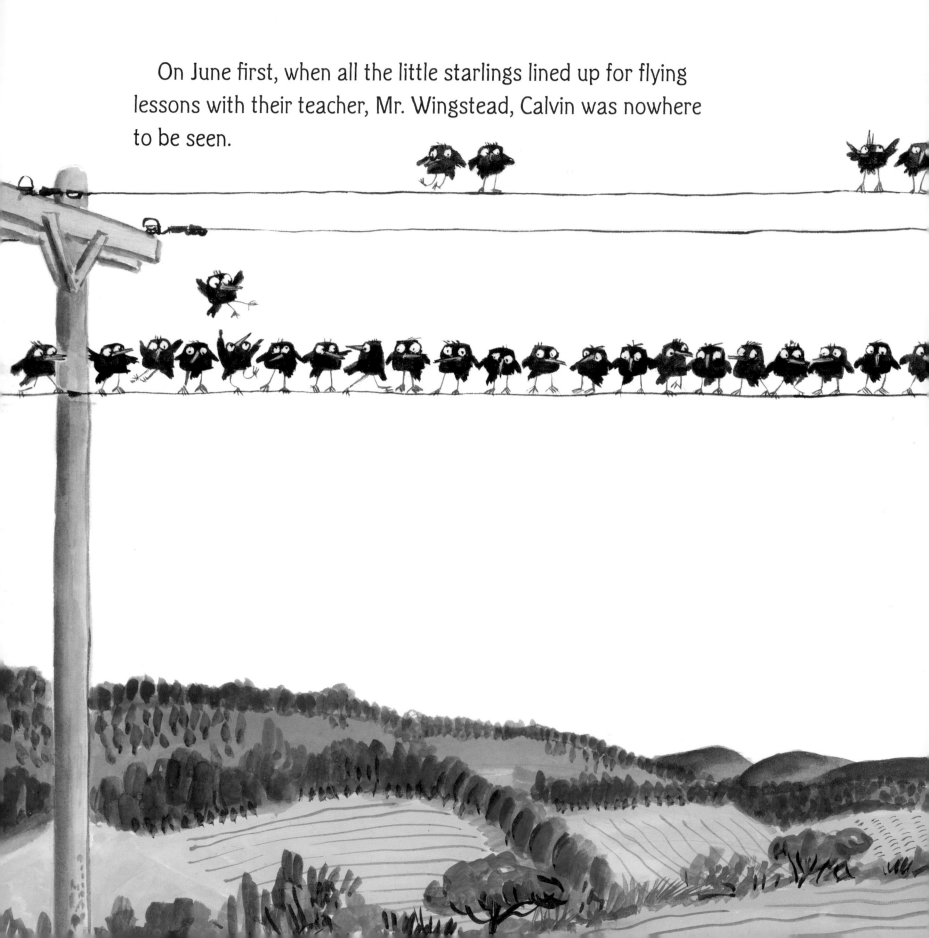

"Where is that bird?"

Actually, Calvin was in the library.

As the other little starlings were learning to SWOOP and HOVER and FLY figure eights, Calvin buried his beak in books.

And there his mind soared.

Calvin read about pirates and cavemen . . .

Volcanoes and rainbows . . .

Whales and dinosaurs . . .

Calvin especially loved dinosaurs!

He learned how the planets circle the sun, what makes the wind blow, and amazing facts, like how caterpillars grow up to become butterflies.

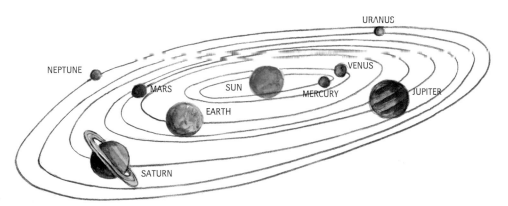

URANUS

NEPTUNE

VENUS

MARS   SUN

MERCURY   JUPITER

EARTH

SATURN

His books took him to places wings never could. And his heart fluttered with excitement.

Calvin's cousins called him

"nerdy birdie,"

"geeky beaky,"

and "bookworm."

And when you're a bird, being called a "worm" is a very bad thing.

Calvin ruffled his feathers and mumbled, "Oh, how the wounding words of scorn do sting!"

Then he sadly waddled back to the library— the only place where he was happy.

And so he spent all summer reading, learning,
and absorbing everything his little starling mind could . . .

. . . until the first leaf turned orange and fell to the ground.

The fall winds sent a chill through the old barn. Summer's nests blew to the floorboards. It was time to head south.

His cousins warned, "Calvin, you better learn to fly. In a couple of days we've got to be out of here!"

Calvin said, "Ah yes, migration. I've read about that."

His sister asked, "Calvin, can you fly?"

Calvin had to admit, he couldn't.

All the other starlings took off in a giant formation. But Calvin could only stand and watch. A big, lonely tear rolled down his cheek.

Calvin turned and trudged back toward the old barn. He was so upset he didn't even notice his brothers and sisters and cousins coming back to get him!

All of a sudden, they were tying up Calvin's middle with string and scraps of cloth they had found in the garbage.

They grasped the other ends with their beaks, and off they flew . . .
with Calvin, somewhat embarrassed, safely in tow.

For days and days they flew.

Calvin recognized the rivers, mountains, and towns he had read about all summer. Excitedly, he pointed them out to his brothers, sisters, and cousins. But the other little starlings just flapped their wings and headed south.

Soon there came a day when the winds blew especially hard. Trees bent sideways. Leaves scattered wildly. Flying became harder and harder. The air had an odd smell to it . . . the smell of DANGER!

Calvin, remembering back to his favorite weather book, warned the rest of his family . . .

"A HURRICANE! A hurricane is coming!"

All his brothers and sisters and cousins asked, "What's a hurricane?"

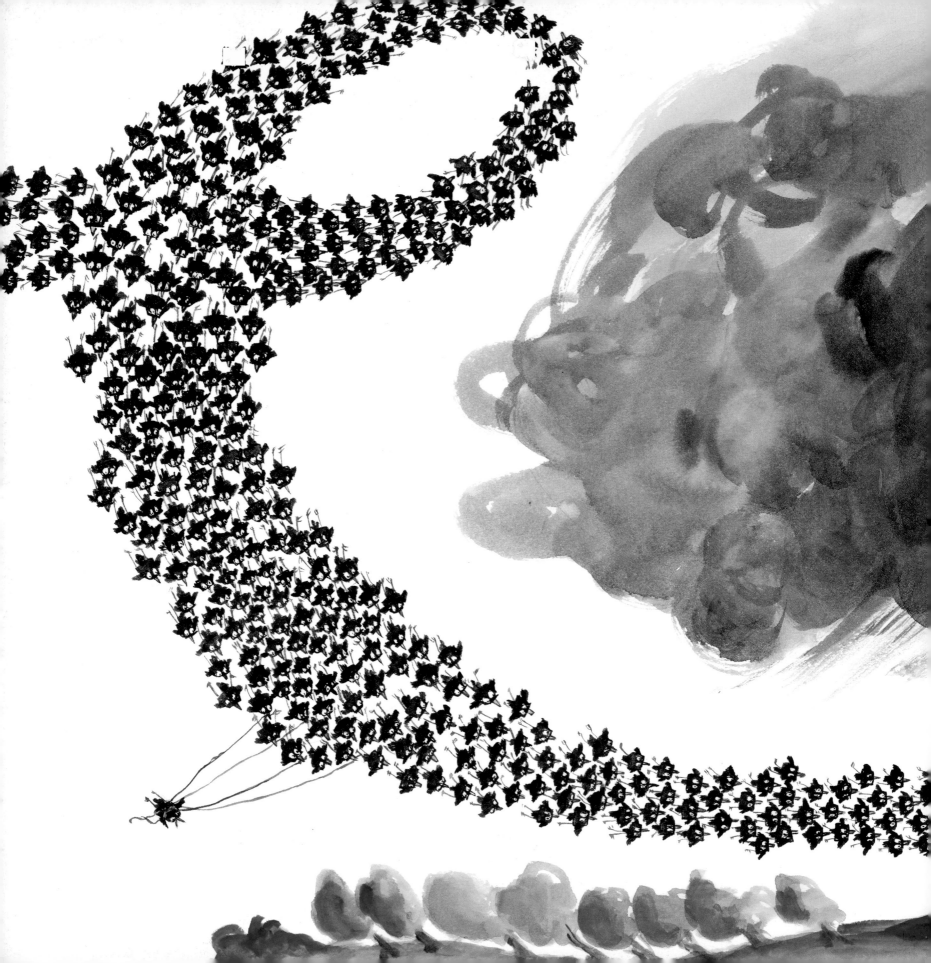

Calvin explained—as quickly as his little beak could—"We need to get out of the path of a violent, tropical weather system, which is storming up the coast at a tremendous speed and will not diminish until it encounters large stretches of landmass! Everybody, make haste, into that cave!"

They had no idea what Calvin was saying. But they had to admit—it did sound real. So, the flock made a loop-de-loop left, a dipsy-doodle right, and dove into the cave. They did everything Calvin told them to.

To their amazement, a great storm did blow across the land.
It thundered over the mountains. It roared through the villages.
It smashed and crashed. Rumbled and raged. Just as Calvin
had predicted.

The whole, big starling family gathered together,
watching in fear and awe.

The storm finally ended. The sun came out in the sky. And the starlings came out of their cave.

They were safe and sound. All because of Calvin.

They celebrated with a great starling party in honor of Calvin.
They ate big, juicy worms and yummy, crunchy beetles. They danced
and sang songs about how Calvin had saved their lives. They toasted
Calvin with acorn caps filled with fresh, clear mountain water.

Calvin was so happy, and felt so good deep down inside, that he jumped and hopped and danced and flapped his wings. . . .

And flapped his wings.

And flapped his wings.

All the other starlings looked at him in amazement.

"Calvin, you can fly!" they exclaimed.

And Calvin, the happiest starling in the whole wide world, chirped, "Why, yes, I do believe I can!"

flap!

flap!

flap!

And they all flew south with big, wide smiles on their little starling faces.

Especially CALVIN.

Just like Calvin, *Jennifer Berne* loves spending time alone with her favorite books about science, nature, cavemen, dinosaurs, and our amazing universe. Unlike Calvin, Jennifer has been a longtime contributor to *Nick Jr.* magazine and a writer for both print and TV. Her recent award-winning picture book, *Manfish: A Story of Jacques Cousteau,* is one of Calvin's favorites.

Keith Bendis is a cartoonist and illustrator whose work has appeared in many of America's leading magazines and newspapers, including the *New Yorker, Vanity Fair, Fortune,* and *Time.* Keith illustrated William Safire's "On Language" column in the *New York Times Magazine* as well as nine books, including the best-selling *Casey at the Bat. Calvin Can't Fly* is his first children's book. Keith lives on an old farm in Columbia County, New York, where he watches starlings fly dipsy-doodles over his house.

For Nick, with whom I happily share my nest. – J.B.

For Kevin and Tadd, two friends who always loved books. – K.B.

STERLING CHILDREN'S BOOKS
New York

An Imprint of Sterling Publishing
387 Park Avenue South
New York, NY 10016

Text © 2010 by Jennifer Berne
Illustrations © 2010 by Keith Bendis
The illustrations in this book were created using gouache.

Designed by Roberta Pressel
Hand lettering by Georgia Deaver

ISBN 978-1-4027-9728-6

Distributed in Canada by Sterling Publishing
c/o Canadian Manda Group, 165 Dufferin Street
Toronto, Ontario, Canada M6K 3H6
Distributed in the United Kingdom by GMC Distribution Services
Castle Place, 166 High Street, Lewes, East Sussex, England BN7 1XU
Distributed in Australia by Capricorn Link (Australia) Pty. Ltd.
P.O. Box 704, Windsor, NSW 2756, Australia

For information about custom editions, special sales, and premium and corporate purchases,
please contact Sterling Special Sales at 800-805-5489 or specialsales@sterlingpublishing.com.

Printed in China
Lot #:
2 4 6 8 10 9 7 5 3 1
09/11

www.sterlingpublishing.com/kids